Carmen's E-Mail

written by Alejandro Segovia
illustrated by Barbara Roman

McGraw-Hill
School Division

New York   Farmington

Carmen Menéndez sat by the window, waiting for her mother to come home from the fast-food restaurant. Finally, Carmen saw her family's blue minivan pull into the driveway. She ran to greet her mom.

"Did you get it, did you get it?" Carmen asked, jumping up and down.

"Yes, Carmen, I got it," Mrs. Menéndez said.
"Here you are—an O'Malleyland Smiley Meal."

"Thanks so much, Mom!" Carmen said.

In one quick motion, she ripped open the
box and pulled out a small stuffed animal.

"A Teeny Tyke tiger!" Carmen squealed. She hugged the soft stuffed tiger to her chest.

"This makes twenty-four Teeny Tykes," Carmen explained. "Now I have more than Mary Brewer, and next week there will be another new one. But this one will definitely be my favorite!" Carmen held her brand-new tiger out to admire it. Then she noticed that something was not quite right.

"What's wrong?" Mrs. Menéndez asked.

"This tiger doesn't have any eyes or nose," Carmen said with a frown. "How can they possibly try to sell faceless Teeny Tykes?"

"Hmm, maybe you should complain to someone about this," said Mrs. Menéndez. "Why don't you write to the company that makes them?"

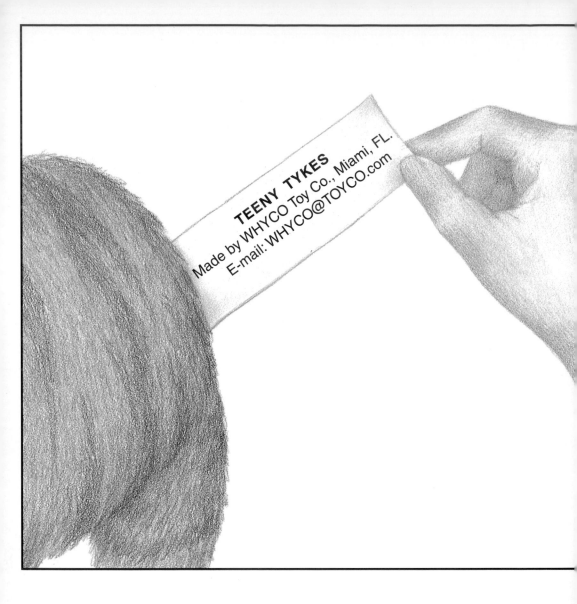

TEENY TYKES
Made by WHYCO Toy Co., Miami, FL.
E-mail: WHYCO@TOYCO.com

"I sure will," Carmen said as she examined the tag on her tiger. "It says Teeny Tykes are made by Whyco Toys, and that the company is right here in Miami. Oh, and here is their e-mail address. I think I'm going to send them a message right now."

Carmen logged on to the family computer
and began to type:

Write Mail

To: WHYCO@TOYCO.com

Subject: TEENY TYKE TIGERS

PRESIDENT OF THE WHYCO TOY COMPANY: HOW
CAN YOU MAKE TEENY TYKE TIGERS
WITHOUT FACES? I WOULD LIKE YOU
TO TAKE ACTION AS SOON AS POSSIBLE
I RECEIVED ONE TODAY AND I'M REALLY NOT
HAPPY WITH IT. THANK YOU.
CARMEN MENENDEZ

"There. That should do it," Carmen said.

The next day, Carmen raced home from school to check her e-mail. There was a reply from Whyco Toys waiting for her. It read:

To: John Smith, President of Whyco Toys

From: The Manufacturing Department

We received your request to make faceless tigers. We are not sure why you want them, but we will follow your orders and start producing them at once.

"They've gotten this completely wrong!" cried Carmen. "Somebody at Whyco Toys thinks I'm the president of the company. For some reason they think I want them to make faceless tigers."

Carmen quickly wrote another letter, explaining who she was and what had happened. She sent the letter and hoped for a speedy reply. A few minutes later, a message came for her.

"Another message for John Smith!" she said. This one was from the Whyco Toys Shipping Department, which said they had already sent out 10,000 faceless tigers.

"What is going on?" Carmen cried.

She wrote a third letter, begging them to understand that she was just an eight-year-old girl who got a faceless tiger by mistake. She wasn't John Smith, president of Whyco Toys, and she never wanted anybody to make 10,000 tigers without faces. Carmen e-mailed the message and sighed. "I hope they get this one right."

Carmen checked her e-mail the next morning and waiting there was a new message from Whyco Toys. It read:

To: John Smith

From: Public Relations

The faceless tigers were a great idea. They are sure to become very valuable. In no time, all the newspapers will be calling for stories. Your idea was pure genius!

Carmen slumped down in her chair, feeling like a 50-pound weight was pressing on her head. "I don't believe this is happening," she said. Beginning to feel frustrated, she typed out one last message.

"To John Smith, President, Whyco Toys— I don't understand how this happened. Why is it that everyone thinks I'm you? All I ever wanted was a Teeny Tyke tiger with a face."

When Carmen got home that afternoon, a long black car was parked on the street. A tall man in a blue suit climbed out of the back seat.

"Are you Carmen Menéndez?" the man asked politely.

"Y-yes, I am," Carmen replied.

"I'm John Smith. I think you know who I am."

"You're the president of Whyco Toys," she said.

"As you might have guessed, we've had some communication problems at Whyco Toys."

Carmen nodded in agreement.

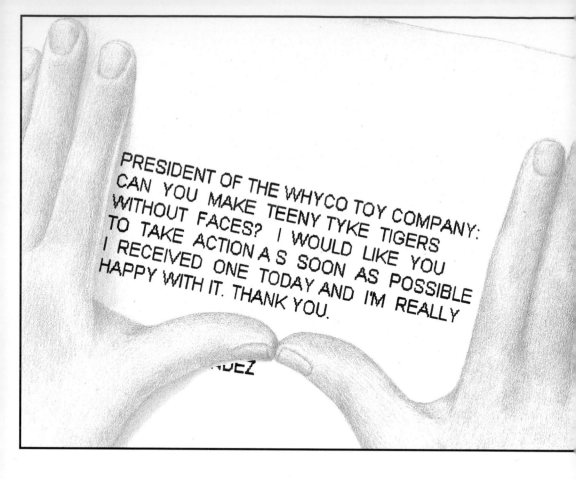

PRESIDENT OF THE WHYCO TOY COMPANY:
CAN YOU MAKE TEENY TYKE TIGERS
WITHOUT FACES? I WOULD LIKE YOU
TO TAKE ACTION AS SOON AS POSSIBLE
I RECEIVED ONE TODAY AND I'M REALLY
HAPPY WITH IT. THANK YOU.

...DEZ

"And now we have 10,000 tigers without faces."

"I'm sorry," Carmen said quietly.

"It's not your fault," Mr. Smith said. "Sometimes computers make mistakes and sometimes humans do. The man who received your first e-mail didn't see the whole message. His window was closed just enough to cut off your name and two important words."

He showed Carmen what he was talking about.

Then he said, "Actually, the faceless tigers have become very popular. We'll probably end up making more, and maybe even a few other faceless animals."

"But I wanted a little tiger with a face," Carmen said.

"I know," Mr. Smith said with a big grin. "I finally got your last message, which is the reason I am here."

He led Carmen and Mrs. Menéndez to the back of the car and had the driver open the trunk.

The trunk of the long black car was filled with all kinds of Teeny Tykes animals.

"Is one of them for me?" Carmen asked.

Mr. Smith shook his head. "They're all for you, Carmen."

Carmen's eyes lit up. "Thanks, Mr. Smith," she said, picking up a Teeny Tyke tiger—one with two shiny black eyes, a button nose, and a mouth.

"You're more than welcome," Mr. Smith answered.

Carmen smiled. "I guess sometimes mistakes turn out all right in the end."